My Mafioso Stepbrothers' Enemy (My Mafioso Stepbrother #2)

Chapter 1

I was in absolute bliss the next few days. I couldn't believe that the whole time, Tommy my step-brother had the same feelings for me that I had for him. It seemed too good to be true. Instead of the hate and loathing I felt from him, all the rage and disinterest, all was because he was trying to protect me. Our family had a lot of enemies', too many to count. Tommy Sicardo was a main man in the Italian mafia. Almost everyone wanted him dead or at the very least arrested. I get butterflies just thinking about my eighteenth birthday. After the cake was eaten and the presents unwrapped, I got my real present Tommy. His dick tasted just as magnificent as it was. Tommy ended up going down on me until I had multiple orgasms', until I had not one but two! He said he wanted to wait a few days to have actual sex. He wanted me to make sure that this is the life that I wanted. I was sure, but I was also the virgin.

Tommy, I don't even want to know how many women he has been with, so I push it out of my mind just the constant danger I'm in especially once people outside this house find out me and Tommy are an item. Tommy basically kept me locked away at boarding school or on vacations to keep me away from his enemies'. To keep me safe.

I am Katherine Sicardo and
this is my story.

Chapter 2

I take the stairs up two at
a time up to my bedroom to
find a single sheet of paper

laying on my desk near my bedroom window. It is a list simple and short but direct nonetheless.

Katherine these are rules period. There will be severe consequences if you even try to bend one. Remember that, Tommy.

1- You will ALWAYS leave this house with a guard.

2- The guard will accompany you everywhere and I mean EVERYWHERE

3- Always let me know where you are going and what time you are to be back. I don't care if it's a fucking gas station.

4- No sneaking out

5- Have your phone on you at all times

6- Don't even think of glancing another man's way or he will die.

So this is it. The last one had a cartoonish drawing of a man slicing another man's throat although, I don't doubt for one minute that he was joking. I guess this is Tommy Sicardo trying to lighten the mood. I guess this is what he was talking about making sure I really understood what been in a relationship with him meant. Guards every single time that I would leave the house. I doubt I would like the consequences; I've seen him mad and mad at me. So, I will need to start learning to live by the rules. Too bad I'm a rule breaker.

Candice, Tommy's want to be girlfriend tried showing up today, this time I wasn't so timid. I more than happily showed her where to go. And I told her not to dare come around here anymore because Tommy was with me now. She tried to yell Tommy around me but I just stepped in her line of vision and showed her the door again. I know he had already told her on the phone but she was adamant I'll give her that. But I really wish I would have had a camera to catch the nasty scowl she gave me the one-time Tommy did appear over my shoulder and pointed at the door himself. She left ranting and raving of choosing "her over me" meaning her perfect body which she did have I'll give her that but Tommy had already had the conversation with her on the phone several times as his phone would not stop ringing for the last two days. Tommy had been extremely busy at work the last couple days so I haven't even seen him much. I still sleep in my room as not all of the household staff is even in on it yet and we are still getting to know each other as well.

"Did you get it?" Tommy asked

"The list?" I could only assume because I haven't received anything else.

"Yes, I don't need to remind you Katherine how important those rules are. Especially now when word is somehow staring to get out already."

"Tommy, I" started

"No! No discussion! Tommy interrupted "This is just a starting list. We will learn and add to it as we discover flaws in the system."

"flaws?" I asked

"Flaws" Tommy said and walked over to me and put his mouth to mine for a slow sensual kiss "I never did punish you for sneaking out to the bar the other night, did I? He asked

"I" stammered as I started to tremble, knowing his rage and backing up until I couldn't back up anymore as my bedroom door was at my back.

"You're scared Katherine" he said it more as a statement on as a question

"Tommy I'm sorry", tears pricked my eyes "how did you even find me?"

"I own that bar Katherine, just like I own the majority of the local police, so keep that in mind." He smirked

"I'm teasing Katherine, I'm not going to hurt you.

I started to let the tension drain from me when he grabbed me by the neck lightly and kissed me passionately as he led my body to the bed and started to undress me. I stayed quiet as I was out of my league So I just let him guide me to where he wanted me and how he wanted me and allowed him to undress me piece by piece silently senior prayer that I had just shower an hour ago. He had me bent over the bed with my thong in-between my ankles stretched tight. He stepped back and admired the view. My nerves were getting the better of me as I heard him undo his belt buckle but then I heard his pants hit the floor along with it. I started to draw a sigh of relief but then his hand was on my pussy and playing with my clit and then slipped one finger than two into me. If I wasn't careful, I was going to come right here and now. As soon as my fluids were good and gushing, he withdrew his fingers and I felt his rock-hard glorious cock demanding entry. It was huge and at first hurt but after a few seconds the hurt turned into immense pleasure as Tommy stood over me rocking his hips. I started to have an orgasm almost immediately and surprisingly so did he.

"God baby, it's been a long time since I've had something so fresh and tight like you are." He dipped his fingers down and grabbed some of our combined juices and told me to suck on his fingers. I did and it was heavenly! I couldn't believe I just lost my virginity! I couldn't believe that Tommy Sicardo came within a few minutes! A man that has been with God only knows how many women. We lay on my bed spent

"Are you ok Katherine?"

"Yes Tommy", is all I could murmur cradled up to his chest breathing him in and memorizing every part of him that I could.

"I've been thinking about this very moment for an extremely long time Katherine." He stated

"Me too" I said and we drifted off to sleep together with me wrapped in those huge biceps and glistening six pack abs for the first time, I was content.

I wore Up early the next
morning with Tommy still
sleep in my bed I quietly
walked until it bathroom
and turned on hot water
and got under the shower it
felt good to have the
steaming hot water hitting
my skin I was still amazed
that I just lost my virginity
last night to a m as n most
women would love to have,
when the door to the
shower opened and Tommy

stood there naked in all of his glory. His Cock was swollen and ready for another release. Tommy stepped under the steaming water with me as we lathered each other all up. He then started to shampoo my hair and then with his hands guided me down in my knees in front of him. He dick was massive and begging to be released! I started putting the enormous cock in my mouth, eyes closed and was enjoying all the sensations as my pussy throbbed and started getting slick between my legs. Tommy fisted my hair pulling down hard so I would have to look at him, his giant cock still in my mouth.

"Look at me Katherine when you duck my cock" Tommy ordered "I love looking into your innocent eyes as you suck my huge cock."

So, with that, I left my eyes open and did what I was told. When he was getting close, my eyes started to droop from ecstasy and a slight tap on my cheek reminded me to open my eyes and watch him as he came into my mouth. I swallowed every last bit, not needing to be told. It was delicious and satisfying and next thing I knew; he had lifted me up and was carrying me to the bed. He played me down gently before pushing his cock deep inside me and fucking me hard for several minutes until me and him came together this time. I never knew what shear ecstasy was until this very moment!

Chapter 3

Luckily Tommy started coming around to Drew and Theresa. He still wasn't exactly thrilled about me being around Drew but he did understand that Theresa was my best friend. That at least he wouldn't take away from me. Last night Theresa and her brother Drew stopped by.

Tommy had just gotten out of the shower and I'm sure purposely strode around the house shirtless. Tommy kept acting as if he was busy working but it wasn't lost on me that he was constantly hovering around us. I thought it was cute. In a million years, I never thought I would he the one to make Tommy Sicardo jealous. It was more than flattering , I couldn't help the smiles that kept creeping onto my face. Of course Tommy now knows I never really wanted Drew, I wanted Tommy but that doesn't stop the way Drew looks at me or the glances Tommy gives him. It's a bit awkward so the visit doesn't last too long. Me and Theresa are planning to meet up in the next few days and spend some time together just us besties.

I'm heading out to the mall this afternoon. Tommy let me go after I promised Tommy that I would play no games and that I would take Bruno one of his head guards with me. I was going to meet Theresa there and I was really excited about that because I haven't seen her in a few days now. Theresa had just started working at a store in the mall and her shift was almost over. Bruno, a man of few words drove me silently to the mall as I texted Theresa updates on my phone. Tommy had bought me a new phone since this was one of the main rules, I had to have it on me and check in with him constantly. No more had I walked into the mall and I almost walked right into Candice! My luck, of course! I texted Theresa and told her about Candice and that I didn't need to be followed around and harassed all day by her and that I was leaving and we would meet tomorrow. Theresa agreed that it just wasn't worth it and when her shift ended in ten minutes, she would just drive to my house to visit. Me and Bruno got back in the car, Candice following us the whole way on foot and we started the drive away from her and back to the house. The next thing I knew was a huge white van T-Boned our SUV and then everything went black.

Chapter 4

 I awoke in a dirty, dark, dank basement area with my head still spinning and blood dripping down from off of my forehead I reached up to touch the damage but luckily my head didn't feel too bad. My whole body hurt. I tried to stand up and that's when I noticed I was handcuffed in some sort of a cell. I tried to stand again but I was too woozy to stand with or without the handcuffs and then I drifted back off into the deep dark abyss of sleep. Several hours later I awoke to the sound of a man shouting and then the horrible scrape of a metal tray being pushed against the cement floor and into my cell. I glanced at it briefly it was water and up plain turkey sandwich. I was extremely thirsty but more afraid of the food and water being drugged or worse, poisoned.

"Well, well sleeping beauty is up." A big muscular man with red hair said

"Who…" my throat was so dry. The man unlocked the cage and grabbed the water and took a sip

"The water is fine, drink."
As soon as the man put
down the cup I yanked up
the glass with my
handcuffed hands and
drank greedily.

"Who are you? Why am I
here?"

"I am Patrick O'Malley. The
man said it like I should
know who he was.

"Who are you and why am I
handcuffed here?" I asked

"My father Sean O'Malley is the head of the Irish mafia." He continued, " we have business to discuss with your step-brother or should I say lover ?" the man chuckled

"I don't know anything about Tommy's business."

"No" Patrick stated, " I'm sure you don't. He was smart to hide you away all these years." Your absolutely breathtaking. "

I choked on the last bit of water but said nothing as the man came closer and traced his finger down my arm and was almost to my breast when I yanked on my handcuffs hard. "Don't touch me!" I screamed which resulted in a hard backhand across my right cheek. I screamed out from the pain. The two times

Tommy had hit me have been nothing compared to what the brute just gave me! I could feel my face swelling already!

"I don't understand, you know that I know absolutely nothing about Tommy's business!" I said in a more controlled voice. The man moved fast and before I knew it, he was pulling me up fast and hard by my hand cuffed arms and had me back up against the wall of that dirty, dank cellar or cage of a Room. It was exactly that, a cage.

"I will ask the questions here!" He roared "And you don't need to worry about anything because pretty soon, when I'm ready, your Tommy will know who has you and what he has to do in order to get you back." Patrick finished as he stated playing with a tendril of my hair. It gave me a chill to my bones.

"Don't touch me!" I yelled in his face and tried to yank away from him.

"A girl who likes to fight. Very sexy. I like a challenge. " Patrick said. He grabbed me by my shirt and pushed me hard up against the cement back wall of the cage. He then grabbed me by the throat and held me in place while he used one of his legs to stop my legs from kicking him. He used his other free hand to grab my breast roughly over my shirt while looking me in my eyes making sure I knew who was in charge.

"I will do or have anything I want, little one." Patrick said in an almost cooing voice. He reached over and purposely touched my body just to show he could. He ran his hands roughly over my breasts and between my legs. No matter how much I squirmed or tried to move my body away, I couldn't. I was absolutely terrified and trapped. I had never been with anyone but Tommy. I was terrified that Patrick was going to rape me. He pushed his hand under my shirt and my bra twisting my right nipple hard and then my left. He unzipped my Jean's and started shoving his hand down my pants to my center. I started crying and begging for him to stop. I was a complete and utter mess. Finally after what seemed forever but was probably only a few seconds, Patrick withdrew. This whole time he had been looking me in my eyes and it wasn't lost on me when he pressed into my leg so I could feel how hard his cock was while he groped me and touched my most private areas against my will. I was on the verge of defeat. I was starting to feel hopeless but when Patrick grinded against me, I felt it. I was pissed. I was beyond pissed. He is a sick fuck, I thought to myself. Patrick must have been at least twice my age and he obviously gets off on forcing young women, extremely young women against their will. I felt defiant in that moment. He was going to take what he wanted with or without my approval or my consent. It didn't matter to him. He was a man who took what he wanted in life and to hell with whomever stood in his way. So I said what I wanted to say and damn the consequences.

"Tommy will kill you and I will enjoy watching him do it pervert" I spat in his face which resulted first in him laughing at me, as if what I just said was the funniest joke he had ever heard. Then the second consequence was another back-hand hit to my face and Patrick still chuckling as he picked up the poor excuse for a sandwich took it with him. I didn't care about eating. I felt sick, absolutely sick to my stomach. As soon as I knew he was gone I wept. I couldn't believe that this had happened to me. I couldn't believe that I was licked in a cage of a monster. I couldn't believe that he almost raped me and that he had pawed all over me and grinded on me. I followed all of Tommy's rules and I made sure I had a body guard with me. Oh my God, Bruno. Where was he? I thought as my hope faded and I shivered a deep body racking shiver in the cool damp hard cement of the cell that had now become my life. I was almost positive if Bruno wasn't already dead he would be so soon. I need to get out of here. I look around for something on the floor,

anything that I could use
the next time Patrick comes
in here but of course, not a
thing besides some dirt and
damp cement is to be found
in my cage.

Tommy

Where in the fuck was
Katherine? It had been an
ambush ! Someone took
what was mine! Katherine!
And I did not share my

property. Whoever the fuck it was, I'm going to RIP out their fucking throat! I had all of my men on it, every single last one of them! I feel so helpless, just like when my father and Katherine's mother were murdered. I had to get her back. Katherine was MINE!

Chapter 5

I awoke sometime later
hearing drops of water
hitting the floor somewhere

in the distance. I couldn't really see; it was almost pitch black. That Patrick man had switched on a light when he had come in but he also made sure to switch it off when he left. I had no sense of time. I could have been there minutes or hours. I tried to wiggle my wrists again and again only causing the skin on my wrists to become more raw and more sore then they already had been but I couldn't just sit here and do nothing. I ended up drifting back off to sleep only to be awoken again by a loud noise when Patrick accompanied by an older man with him unlocked the cage I was in and turned on the light.

 "Patrick this is no way to treat a guest" The man spoke.

"Come here my dear let me help you up, my name is Sean. Sean O'Malley". Sean motioned to Patrick and Patrick supplied him with a key to my handcuffs and I watched him curiously as the father undid my handcuffs and helped me up into a standing position.

"Son," Sean spoke to the younger man, "how would you like it if one of our friends say did this to your sister? I don't think neither one of us would take this too kindly." He remarked

"Whatever you say dad." Patrick answered

"Son, go get me a glass of water and a ice pack for this young lady." Sean continued in almost a soothing voice but I had to remember that because of this man, I was literally imprisoned. It was Tommy's worst nightmare, and it came true all too quickly. "Ms.,"

"My name is Katherine. " I answered " And I want to go home! Whatever you and Tommy have going on, it doesn't involve me." I finished annoyed and angry

"I would like for you to join us for dinner. I will provide you with a shower and evening attire." Sean said ignoring my demands to be released and to go home. He motioned to a guard who had been standing relatively close and the guard nodded his head and proceeded to take me lightly by my arm walk me out of my cell. I try to take in as much of my surroundings as possible as I was guided through what seemed like a huge dark and damp basement of some sort of a warehouse setting as I was led down a long hallway and up a long stretch of stairs. The stairs were creaky and steep. If not for the guards flashlight, I wouldn't have been able to see anything. I could just start to make out some light at the top of the stairs. The guard opened the door and we walked up the last step into a house. It was a huge mansion not a warehouse at all. I had never seen a house so big. It made Tommy's house seem like a shack. There were numerous guards milling about and cooks preparing food while maids prepared the table settings at a table that looked to hold at least fourteen people. The house was beautifully decorated with carved ornate wood and masculine colors like navy and forest green. The guard had to give me a slight tug on my arm to keep me from gawking and to keep moving forward up another flight of stairs to the upstairs of the second story house where two long corridors were located both of which had numerous bedrooms and bathrooms to be found. The guard led me into a bedroom and shut the door behind me, firmly locking it in place. I look around frantically for a phone but none are to be found. I ran to the large window to find it had metal bars preventing my escape. I walk into the bathroom figuring st least I could take a shower and get a good meal while I wait for my best chance to run and fight if need be. I step into the streaming hot water feeling all the dirt and grime from however long I was down in the cell of their vast basement wash off. Before to long, I rinsed off and grabbed fresh towels to dry off. As I walk back into the adjoining bedroom, I find someone had placed a evening gown with dress shoes onto the bed along with a small container holding brand new makeup inside and some I assume costume jewelry on the bedside table. I don't know what these people are thinking, my face is still bruised from the sons son's vicious assault and now they want me to play dress-up? These people are absolutely insane ! Nonetheless, I get dressed. I find a blow-dryer in the bathroom and blow dry my hair, apply the makeup and put on the emerald green floor length evening gown. I need to play as long until I can find a way to escape from here. I don't know if father and son are playing good cop, bad cop or what. It doesn't change the fact that I don't know anything about Tommy's business and even if I did, I wouldn't tell a soul. I know Tommy is searching for me and it has to be only a matter of time before the doors on this place getting kicked in and

Tommy reducing me. I have no clue what day it is or how long I've been here, I just remember that we were supposed to be leaving soon, me and Tommy, for our first vacation together in years. A sad pang hits my chest as tears prick st my eyes. I was so looking forward to that trip when I should have just been content on having Tommy. I have to stop my tears and keep my head in the game. I have to either find as way out or bide my time until Tommy can find me and rescue me himself. I would much rather go along with the fathers way of playing dress-up than the sons way. I get chills just thinking about Patrick's hands on me.

A short time later there was a knock at the door. It was the guard from earlier ready to get me for dinner. He grabbed me lightly by the arm again and led me out of the room, down the long corridor, down the stairs and into the dining room with the massive dining room table. He walked me over to my seat and I sat down. Sitting at the huge, oversized dining room table was only two other occupants, Patrick and Sean. This is going to be an extremely awkward experience, I thought to myself. Play along Katherine, just bide your time.

As the mains finish putting out the dinnerware and the cook started serving out the soup, everyone acted as if I wasn't a kidnapped prisoner being held here against my will. Everyone ignored me completely! Not a single person would even glance in my direction so I doubted very much if I screamed for help that any of them would do anything. I wondered if this was a common occurrence here, that a kidnapped prisoner was made to eat supper like they were friends or a family member just visiting for the day. Or maybe they were just too scared themselves to do anything.

My silent thoughts were interrupted as Sean, the oldest O-Malley cleared his throat.

"You look absolutely stunning Katherine." He said

"Um, thank you." I replied thinking about the bruising that was still highly evident on my face despite half of a stick of concealer trying to hide it. There was a knock at the door.

"Ah, yes our last guest has arrived." Sean said pleased with himself. I was praying it was Bruno but the sinister way Sean was looking toward the door showed me I wasn't going to like who this "guest" was. I looked up from my soup and was shocked to see who it was.

Chapter 6

"Candice!" I almost spit out the mouthful of soup all over the table when I saw her walking in while dressed in her evening attire. Sean and Patrick both got up from their seats and kissed her on her cheek and then Sean held out a chair for her across from me. Sean was on one end of the massive table and Patrick on the other.

"Hello Katherine." She said as if this was just another normal day in a normal setting. So she set me up ! I should have known it! She was at the mall and she was beyond pissed that Tommy didn't want anything to do with her. She was getting me out of the picture! I could have gotten up and choked her to death right there and then!

"What is this?!" I demanded

"Candice is a good friend of the family's." Sean answered as if introducing me to her for the first time.

"Candice, you did this to me? To Tommy?" I asked dumbfounded

"No, Tommy did this to you when he broke up with me." Candice answered so high up on her horse it made me hate her even more

"Why?" "How could you?" I continued "Tommy will never want you now." I said

"He hasn't wanted me since you came back from school, early I might add." Candice stated

"So this is your revenge? To get me kidnapped, imprisoned?" I spat. The senior O'Malley cleared his throat

"Now, now girls. Let's enjoy our dinner and leave the sparing for later. He chuckled

And so the dinner went. Like it was an everyday, small talk, nonchalant dinner. It was extremely bizarre and I sat there picking at my food. Don't get me wrong, the food was absolutely delicious and cooked to perfection. And the whole affair would have been a classy one, if one of the attendees wasn't there by force. At one point I tried telling Candice she could still stop this but I was cut off sternly by the senior O'Malley. That was the only time I saw a trace of anger in his features. Otherwise he was the perfect host, picking out wines to pair with each course, and even trying to make a joke about providing alcohol to an underage meaning me since I had only recently turned eighteen. But I guess what's it to him providing alcohol to a minor when he has kidnapping and forced imprisonment already going for him. Not once did Tommy's business come up so I'm not sure why I was even included in this charade of a dinner except to inform me that Candice was to blame for my current position. I kept glancing around here and there looking for doors and un-barred windows but to no avail. The curtains were drawn but I did notice that when they did answer the door for Candice earlier that they had a key to unlock the big oak front door from inside the house. I'm sure I would be correct to assume every door and window is locked from the inside or has bars on it and that I'm just trapped in a bigger prison. After dinner, I was led back up to my room where s fresh pair of pajamas lay out on the bed. I washed off my face making sure to get all the makeup off and put on the cashmere pajamas and crawled into bed. I was silently thanking God that at least I got to sleep in a bed tonight instead of that dark, dank cellar cage although I'm still not sure what day it is or how long I've been here. I pray Bruno wasn't taken but if he was then I hope they are not torturing him somewhere. I say a silent prayer for Bruno's safety and make a mental note to ask, no demand some answers tomorrow. I know should have today but the whole bizarre situation of being beaten and then today let out of the cage in the basement to attend a formal evening dinner through me off my end game which is to get the hell out of here. After what seemed like hours, I was startled awake by the sound of keys unlocking my door. I could see through the drapes that it was still dark outside so I knew they weren't coming for me to eat breakfast. I heard the door creak open and I immediately sat up in bed fully awake. The hallway was dark so I couldn't see who was coming into the room that had become my new prison. The senior O'Malley seemed to have much more sense and class than the younger one, but I was still terrified of them both equally. Just because Sean had allowed me out of the cage, a fresh shower and formal attire along with a sit down meal, it didn't mean I trusted him anymore than I trusted his son, Patrick.

"Hello?" I asked but no one answered. The door closed and locked but I knew I wasn't alone. I could hear the footsteps as they got closer to my bed. I reached over and turned on the bedside lamp as fast as I could and then I screamed.

Chapter 7

It was Patrick. He was in my bedroom and had locked himself in here with me. No more had I started to scream and he clamped a large hand over my mouth. I tried to bite him and started to fight him. He pushed me down on the bed with all of his weight and told me to shut up. I couldn't breathe with his hand covering my mouth and nose. I thought I was going to pass out. He kept telling me to shut up and to stop screaming. I was absolutely terrified. He was on top of me now. He was using his body to pin my body down. He still wouldn't remove his hand that was covering my mouth and nose. Everything was starting to get blurry.

My lungs felt as if they were on fire as all the oxygen in my body was depleted.

This was it, I thought. He's going to rape me. No, God no. I started seeing white spots in my vision. I'm going to pass out or he's going to kill me and rape me. I have never been as terrified as I was right now in this moment. This is it. This is how I'm going to die.

Patrick started pawing at

my night clothes. He was trying to push my pajama bottoms off while still not allowing me to breathe. I was going to lose this fight and fast, I thought. He pulled up my shirt and roughly started fondling my breasts. He then tried a second time now that I was weaker to pull down my pants. He almost had my pants and underwear off as I started to black out from lack of oxygen. All of the sudden, I heard some very loud commotion out in the hallway. Patrick cursed and then let go of me all of the sudden. He quickly got up and in a few strides he was back at the door and he unlocked the door and left the room to see what the commotion was. I sat up gasping for air, choking. Next thing I knew was I heard Patrick yelling and cursing at one of the maids who had knocked over something on her way to the restroom. I sat there stunned for a minute, collecting my bearings. I then looked around the room for something, anything I could use as a weapon if he came back. I couldn't find much but the blow-dryer in the bathroom that maybe I could hit him over the head with bit it was better than nothing at all. I knew I wasn't going to go back to sleep. I was going to sit on my bed and wait armed with the blow-dryer and ready to defend myself. On my way back over to sit on the bed, I caught one of my toes on the chair that sat at the simple desk. I dropped the blow-dryer and pulled the wooden chair over to my door and tilted it backwards

and under the door handle
to prevent the door from
being opened key or no key.
I then grabbed the blow-
dryer and sat on my bed. I
could tell from looking at
the door to the hallway that
all the lights had been
turned back off. I sat there
for what seemed like
forever until I finally heard
it. Someone was trying to
unlock my door and come
in. I started shaking with

fear, clutching the blow-dryer with both hands and preparing myself for a fight when I heard it. It was a hushed whisper of a women. I hurried up and dropped the blow-dryer and ran over to the door to take the wooden chair away. I hesitated only briefly wondering if I was being set-up. I took the chair away and opened the door. The oldest one of the few maids I saw earlier dressing the dinner table was there. She looked like a grandmother. I remembered trying to get her to look at me but none of the workers would. She pushed me back inside the room and locked the door quickly behind her. She was shushing me the whole time. Then she waited a few moments in silence to make sure the house was quiet before she spoke.

"My name is Evelyn. I'm a maid here." She said in a light whisper continuing, "Patrick is a bad man. He's evil. I'm sorry that we couldn't help you at dinner but I heard him come into your room earlier so I broke a vase in the hallway to try to get him out. I hope I got to you in time." She finished and I just hugged her as tears silently ran down my face on their own accord. I fell apart right then and there in Evelyn's arms. She let me weep onto her shoulder as I shook my head yes all the while she hugged me tight. After a short while she pulled away from me saying that she had to hurry and get back to her room before she was caught. I begged her in hushed tones to please help me and get me out of there. She responded she couldn't because it would mean a certain death for her and as she said that I understood it would be true. If Evelyn were to let me out of the house it would most certainly mean her death and I couldn't bear for this nice grandmotherly woman who saved me from a rapist, for her death to be on my shoulders. I was able

with her help to give her
Tommy's phone number
and asked her if she could
please get a message to him
as to where I was at and
what has been happening
to me. She said that none of
staff are able to come and
go as they please. They are
all contracted workers and
part of the contract was for
all of them to live on the
premises to be at the
O'Malley's back and call at

all hours of the day. She quickly and quietly had unlocked the door Khan back to her Room and came back with a small piece of paper and a pencil as to where I could write down Tommy's phone number and address. She said that the cook would be gone into town the next day to grab fresh seafood for supper and that she would pass the so long. I prayed that the cook would help me however, Evelyn assured me that she would. I was still doubtful that a bunch of women that I have never not once in my life met would all be willing to put their lives on the line to help me get out of this hell. I had no choice but to have faith, faith Tommy would come get me.

The next morning, I awoke to a light knock on

the bedroom door. I must have drifted off as I stayed awake almost all-night waiting for Patrick to come back. It was the same guard from yesterday collecting me for today's breakfast. I grabbed a robe that I noticed was hanging in the bathroom yesterday and pulled it on along with some slippers that had been put out for me. I allowed the guard to gently ide me back out of the room down the long hallway, down the stairs and back to the dining room. Both Patrick and Sean were already seated eating their breakfast on opposite sides of the massive dining room table like they were yesterday. Just like yesterday I was to be seated in the middle of both of them with multiple empty chairs between me and each of them. I didn't know if this was for their protection or if they just liked to flash their money. I expected it to be a little bit of each reason.

"I trust you slept well Katherine. "Sean said

I looked to Patrick and he had the audacity to look and act like nothing had happened and patiently waited for a response out

of me himself. I doubted
the older O'Malley would
believe me if I said anything
or even if he did believe
me, I doubted very much
that he would care. He
probably knew all too well
who his son was and what
he was capable of.

"Um, yes. I slept well." I lied
all the while looking at
Patrick. I knew I looked like
shit. I haven't a spot of
make up on and the

bruising was still obviously evident on my face from Patrick's assault a few days prior along with maybe a few minutes of sleep total.

"Well you're in for a treat tonight!" Sean continued "I had the cook go into town this morning to grab fresh seafood for seafood feast tonight." He finished as if I was just any other guest that had stayed with them. It was weird. The senior

O'Malley treated me almost like a family member! A treat would to be able to go home, back toy own life.

"When can I go home? And where is Bruno? How long have I been here? And what do you plan on doing with me?" I let the questions flow from my mouth not waiting for one answer before asking the next.

This time Patrick spoke, "Don't take my father's manners and grace and throw them in his face. If you want to go back into the cage, you can. Or you can entertain him and act accordingly. "

"Manners and grace ? You tried raping me last night! I was beaten and kept in a cage!" Your father may have manners and grace but I'm still a prisoner here and held against my will!" I shouted. They both just looked at me and then both continued to eat their breakfast without answering any of my questions. Maybe I was better off in the cage. They are both absolutely insane!

"Hello?" I said sarcastically and they both continued to ignore me. I could probably scream and shout but I doubt they would stop eating their breakfast and acknowledge me. I wasn't even shocked that they gentle more senior O'Malley didn't even react when I called out Patrick about trying to rape me last night. These men were used to taking what they want and when they wanted. The senior O'Malley wasn't being kind or gracious to me, he was playing his own sick games. Letting me feel as if I was free when we both knew I was not. I was probably something nicer to look at across the table than only looking at his son. I was his entertainment I wasn't hungry. I wasn't in the mood to play their games. When I refused to order breakfast the guard just reappeared and led me back to the room and locked me in. I just sat on the bed. I should be crying. I

should be a complete mess,
but I was too exhausted
and too angry. I laid down
on the bed still wearing my
pajamas and my robe and
drifted off into a light sleep.
I wasn't asleep very long
before I awoke to chaos
and gunshots.

Chapter 8

I didn't know what was going on. It was early evening by this time as the sun was already starting to set. I rolled off of the bed onto the floor and then proceeded to roll under the bed. I could hear men shouting and what seemed like endless gunfire. Whatever was going on out there, I didn't want to have any part of it.

For the first time in days I felt hope. Maybe the cook got my message to Tommy or maybe Candice had finally come to her senses. But maybe, this was something totally different. I wasn't sure so I stay hidden under the bed through all the shouting and gunfire. It seemed to go on forever! I heard someone trying to come into my room. Whoever it was, they didn't have a key and I was hearing loud noises as if they were trying to kick down my door! I started trembling all over, shaking with fear. Whoever this was didn't belong here. I heard shouting.

"She isn't here!" a voice said. It took me a minute to realize whose voice that was over all the commotion still going on in the lower half of the house. It was Bruno's! Bruno was alive! I yelled out for him under the safety of the bed. I yanked my hand out from under the bed to show him I was here and at the very moment gunfire erupted much much closer this time and I felt a sharp pain in my side. My right side of my rib cage was on fire! And now I was having trouble breathing. I was shot! I knew it and before I could react, I started blacking out. I was terrified one minute and then a calmness washed over me. I knew Bruno was ok and I could hear Tommy yelling but it sounded as if I was under water as I drifted into the dark abyss. I just thought about my mom and Tommy's dad, the one who I eventually called my own.

At least I would be seeing them really soon. At least I would be with my mom. God how I missed her.

The next thing I remember is waking up in a hospital room. When I opened my eyes, I immediately saw Tommy sitting next to me and if there was a way Tommy could not look his best, it was now. But to me he was so beautiful. You could tell he was stressed, as he hadn't shaved in days and he was in wrinkled up, blood soaked clothes. He was deep in thought, tears in his eyes when he noticed I was waking up.

"Katherine!" oh, God Katherine! I thought I had lost you ! I have never been so scared in my entire life! I thought you were gone, like our parents." Tommy said as he teared up.

"What happened?" I asked my voice still course

Tommy explained to me that I had been shot in my right side and my lung had collapsed. I had gone into surgery and I had lost a bunch of blood but the Doctors were eventually able to stabilize me and since then which was two days ago, it had been a waiting game to see when and even if I would wake up. I had been at the O'Malley's house for five days, three of which in a cage. The cook did in fact save me by getting a message to Tommy and he wasted no time getting to me and thus saving me. The senior O'Malley was dead along with the main guard that had led me to and from my meals. All of the O'Malley's workers lived except one that perished in the gunfire. Evelyn made it out safely and so did the cook. I was so happy that they risked their lives to save mine. Sean O'Malley on the other hand, fled. He left his father and his guards to be gunned down and escaped through a hidden tunnel down in that dark, damp basement. By the time Tommy and his men found the tunnel which led to a road a few blocks from the O'Malley's, Sean had been long gone. Tommy did find out that the O'Malley's were responsible for our parents deaths from paperwork found in the O'Malley home. He found contracts and a money trail leading all the way back to when his father and my mother met. It made me sad but at least we had closure. At least we know knew who the enemy was and I knew Tommy would track down Sean and make him pay. I didn't doubt that for a second.

The next few days flew by as I recuperated in the hospital and started physical therapy to gain my strength back. I was able to meet up with Evelyn and the other staff on the day I was being discharged from the hospital. I cried as I hugged each and every one.

None of them had any clue
to where Sean O'Malley
had went but they were just
as happy to be free as I was.
It seemed Sean had a habit
of raping the female staff
whenever he chose but
paid them so little money
that most of the staff
couldn't afford to move out
and leave and the rest of
the staff were just too
afraid of the O'Malley's.
Leave it to Tommy to offer

each and every single one of them jobs and s place to live while they rebuilt their lives, no strings attached. As for Candice, well my brother let me watch as he slit her throat ear to ear and we watched her bleed out together. After what she put me through, because of her all of this mess had happened, I was happy to watch. And to my surprise, we still had a few days before we were scheduled to leave on vacation together. It seemed everything had worked out for now bit when your name is Sicardo , there are so many enemies waiting to take you down and to take what you and your family had built. But for now, I'm content to have a no drama, lots of sex vacation waiting for me.

Till the next time,

Katherine